Penelope Lively

Ghostly Guests

Illustrated by Frank Rodgers

 YELLOW BANANAS

Chapter One

MARIAN AND SIMON were sent to bed early
on the day that the Brown family moved
house. By then everyone had lost their temper
with everyone else. The cat had been sick on
the sitting room carpet and the dog had run
away twice.

If you have ever moved, you will know
what kind of day it had been. There were
packing cases and newspaper all over the
place. There were sandwiches instead of
proper meals. The kettle was lost, a wardrobe
had stuck on the stairs and Mrs Brown's

favourite vase got broken. There was only
bread and baked beans for supper, the
television wouldn't work and the water
wasn't hot.

After all that, the children didn't object too violently to being packed off to bed. They'd had enough, too. They had one last argument about who was going to sleep by the window, then they put on their pyjamas, got into bed and switched the lights out. It was at that point that the ghost came out of the bottom drawer of the chest of drawers.

It oozed out, a grey cloudy shape about
three feet long, smelling faintly of wood-
smoke. Then it sat down on a chair and
began to hum to itself. It looked like a bundle
of bedclothes, except that it was not solid.
You could see, quite clearly, the cushion
on the chair beneath it.

Marian gave a shriek. 'That's a ghost!'

'Oh, be quiet, dear, do,' said the ghost. 'That noise goes right through my head. And it's not nice to call people names.' It took out a ball of wool and began to knit.

What would you have done? Well, Simon
and Marian did just that. You can imagine
what happened next. You try telling your
mother that you can't get to sleep because
there's a ghost sitting in the room clicking
its knitting needles and humming. Mrs Brown
didn't believe a word of it.

The ghost went on knitting and humming and Mrs Brown went out banging the door behind her. 'If there's so much as another word from either of you...' she said.

'She can't see it,' said Marian to Simon.

'Course not, dear,' said the ghost. 'It's you children I'm here for. Love little ones, I do. We're going to be ever such friends.'

'Go away!' yelled Simon. 'This is our house now!'

'No it isn't,' said the ghost smugly. 'Always been here, I have. A hundred years and more. Seen plenty of families come and go, I have. Go to sleep now, there's good children.'

The children glared at the ghost and buried themselves under the bedclothes. Eventually they slept.

Chapter Two

THE NEXT NIGHT the ghost was there again.
This time it was smoking a long white pipe
and reading a newspaper dated 1842. Beside
it was a second grey cloudy shape.

'Hello, children,' said the ghost. 'Say how
do you do to Auntie Edna.'

'She can't come here too,' wailed Marian.

'Oh yes she can,' said the ghost. 'Always
comes here in August, does Auntie. She likes
a change.'

Auntie Edna was even worse, if possible.
She sucked peppermints that smelled so

strong that Mrs Brown looked suspiciously
under the pillows when she came to kiss
Marian and Simon goodnight. Auntie Edna
also sang hymns in a loud squeaky voice.

The two children lay there groaning as the ghosts sang and rustled newspapers and ate peppermints.

The next night there were three of them!
'Meet Uncle Charlie,' said the first ghost. The
children groaned.

'And Jip,' said the ghost. 'Here, Jip, good
dog - come and say hello to the children.'

A large grey dog that you could see straight
through came out from under the bed,
wagging its tail.

The cat, who had been curled up beside Marian's feet, gave a howl and shot on top of the wardrobe, where it sat spitting.

The dog lay down in the middle of the rug and started scratching itself. Maybe it had ghost fleas, the children thought.

Uncle Charlie was unbearable. He had a loud cough that kept going off like a machine gun and he told the longest and most pointless stories the children had ever heard. He said he too loved children and he knew children loved stories. In the middle of the seventh story the children went to sleep out of sheer boredom.

The following week the ghosts left the bedroom and went all over the house. The children had no peace at all. They'd be quietly doing their homework and all of a sudden Auntie Edna would be breathing down their necks reciting arithmetic tables.

The original ghost took to sitting on top
of the television with her legs in front of the
picture. Uncle Charlie told his stories all
through the best programmes and the dog
lay permanently at the top of the stairs.

The Browns' cat became quite nervous. It refused to eat and went to live on the top shelf of the kitchen dresser.

Chapter Three

SOMETHING HAD TO be done. Marian and Simon were beginning to look tired. Their mother decided they looked peaky and bought some sticky brown vitamin medicine from the chemists to strengthen them.

'It's the ghosts!' wailed the children. 'We don't need vitamins!'

Their mother said she didn't want to hear another word of this silly nonsense about ghosts.

Auntie Edna, who was sitting smirking on the other side of the kitchen table at that very moment, nodded vigorously and took out a packet of humbugs which she sucked noisily.

'We've got to get them to go and live somewhere else,' said Marian. But where, that was the problem, and how?

On Sunday the Browns were all going to see their uncle who was rather rich and lived alone in a big house. It had thick carpets everywhere and empty rooms and in one of them was the biggest colour television set you ever saw. Plenty of room for ghosts.

This gave Simon a bright idea. He suggested to the ghosts that they might like a drive in the country. The ghosts said that they were quite comfortable where they were, thank you. They didn't fancy these new-fangled motor-cars, not at their time of life. But then Auntie Edna remembered that she liked looking at pretty flowers and trees.

So they agreed to give it a try.

They sat in a row on the back shelf of the car. Mrs Brown kept asking why there was such a strong smell of peppermint and Mr Brown kept roaring at Simon and Marian to keep still while he was driving.

The fact was that the ghosts were shoving them. It was like being nudged by three cold damp flannels. And the dog, who had come along too, of course, was car sick.

When they got to Uncle Dick's the ghosts came in and had a look round. They liked the expensive carpets and the enormous television. They slid in and out of the wardrobes and walked through the doors and walls. Uncle Dick's budgerigars went crazy and were never the same again.

'Nice place,' the ghosts said. 'Nice and
comfy.'

'Why not stay here?' said Simon.

'Couldn't do that,' said the ghost firmly.

'Too dull. We like a place with a bit of life.'

And they piled back into the car and sang
hymns all the way home to the Browns'
house. When they weren't singing they were
eating the leftover lunch. There were crumbs
all over the car floor and the children got
the blame.

Simon and Marian were in despair. The ruder they were to the ghosts, the more the ghosts liked it. 'Cheeky!' they said. 'Children these days are so bold. They don't care what they say. Not like when we were young and little children were seen and not heard.'

Chapter Four

THE CHILDREN COULDN'T even bath on their own. One or other of the ghosts would come and sit on the taps and talk to them. One day Uncle Charlie had produced a mouth organ and played the same tune over and over again. It was so annoying. The children went around with their hands over their ears.

Mrs Brown took them to the doctor to find out if there was something wrong with their hearing. The children knew better than to say anything to the doctor about the ghosts. It was pointless saying anything to anyone.

I don't know what would have happened if Mrs Brown hadn't made friends with Mrs Walker from down the road. Mrs Walker had twin babies and one day she brought the babies along for tea.

Now one baby is bad enough. Two babies are big trouble. When they weren't both howling, they were crawling around the floor looking for something to play with. They pulled the tablecloths off the tables and bumped their heads on the chairs.

They hauled the books out of the bookcases.

They threw their food all over the kitchen and
flung cups of milk on the floor. Their mother
mopped up after them without complaining.

Every time she tried to sit down and talk to Mrs Brown, the babies bawled in chorus so that no one could hear a word.

In the middle of this the ghosts appeared. One baby was yelling its head off and the other was glueing chewed up bread to the front of the television.

The ghosts swooped down on the babies
with happy cries. 'Oh!' they trilled. 'Bless
their little hearts then. Diddums! Give
Auntie a smile then.'

And the babies stopped in mid-howl and
gazed at the ghosts. The ghosts cooed at the
babies and the babies cooed at the ghosts. The
ghosts chattered to the babies and sang them
songs. The babies chattered back and were as
good as gold for the next hour. Their mother
had the first proper chat she'd had in weeks.

When they went home the ghosts stood in
a row at the window, waving.

Simon and Marian knew what to do now.
That evening they had a talk with the ghosts
about moving in with the Walker twins. At
first the ghosts were not sure this would be
a good idea. They didn't fancy moving. You
get set in your ways at their age, they said.
Auntie Edna reckoned she would never get
used to a strange house.

Simon and Marian didn't give in that easily. They talked about the babies non-stop.

The next day they led the ghosts down the road, followed by the ghost dog, straight into the Walkers' house.

Chapter Five

MRS WALKER DOESN'T know to this day why the babies, who had been screaming for the last half hour, suddenly stopped and broke into great smiles. And she has never understood why, from that day on, the babies became the most well-behaved babies in the area.

The ghosts kept the babies amused from morning to night.

The babies thrived. The ghosts were happy The ghost dog, who was actually a bitch, settled down so well that she had puppies.

That was a surprise!

The Brown children heaved a sigh of relief and got back to normal life. The babies, though, I have to tell you, grew up somewhat peculiar.

Have you enjoyed this Yellow Banana? There are plenty more to read. Why not try one of these exciting new stories:

A Funny sort of Dog *by Elizabeth Laird*

There's something not quite right about Simon's new puppy, Tip. It's very big with long claws, and it climbs trees. Then one day it roars and Simon has to face the truth . . . perhaps Tip isn't a dog at all!

Carole's Camel *by Michael Hardcastle*

Carole is left a rather unusual present – a camel called Umberto. It's great to to ride him to school and everyone loves him, even if he is rather smelly. But looking after a real camel can cause a lot of problems. Perhaps she should find him a more suitable home . . .

The Pony that went to Sea *by K.M. Peyton*

Paddy, an old forgotten pony is adopted by Tom and Emily Tarboy. One stormy night, Paddy is taken aboard the houseboat where the children live. But during the night the boat breaks free and is carried out to sea. It's up to Paddy to save the day.

Ollie and the Trainers *by Rachel Anderson*

Ollie has two problems: he has no trainers and he can't read. Dad agrees to buy him some trainers but they turn out to be no ordinary pair. They are Secret Readers and can talk! Can Leftfoot Peter and Rightfoot Paul help Ollie to read?

Bella's Den *by Berlie Doherty*

Moving to the country, my only friend is Bella. One day she shows me her secret – a den. We go there one night and see some foxes, and in my excitement I blurt out what I've seen and a farmer overhears. He says foxes kill lambs and later he sets off to hunt them down. I've got to stop him . . .